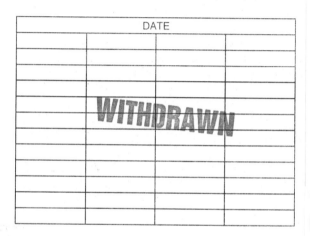

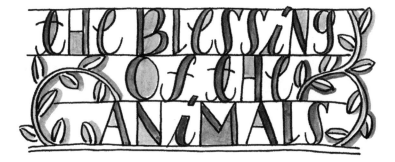

THE BLESSING OF THE ANIMALS

THE BLESSING
OF THE ANIMALS
STORY & PICTURES BY
MICHAEL J. ROSEN

FARRAR STRAUS
GIROUX,
NEW
YORK

We . . . are apt to justify leaving animal welfare aside
on the grounds that human needs are more urgent.
We must hammer home that love is indivisible.
It is not *either-or*; it is *both-and*.
—*Right Reverend John Austin Baker, Bishop of Saintsbury*

Text and illustrations copyright © 2000 by Michael J. Rosen
All rights reserved
Distributed in Canada by Douglas & McIntyre Ltd.
Printed in the United States of America
Typography by Judy Lanfredi
Hand-lettering by Michael J. Rosen
First edition, 2000
1 3 5 7 9 10 8 6 4 2

Library of Congress Cataloging-in-Publication Data
Rosen, Michael J.
    The blessing of the animals / story and pictures by Michael J.
Rosen. — 1st ed.
        p.   cm.
    SUMMARY: Jared must decide if it would be all right for him to take
his dog Shayna to the annual St. Francis Festival at the Catholic Church
near his house, even though he is Jewish.
    ISBN 0-374-30838-1
    1. Jews—United States Fiction.  [1. Jews—United States Fiction.
2. Francis, of Assisi, Saint, 1182–1226—Fiction.   3. Dogs—Fiction.]
I. Title.
    PZ7.R71868   Bl   2000
    [Fic]—dc21                                          99-34323

ACKNOWLEDGMENTS

I would like to extend my gratitude once again to the Ohio Arts Council, which provided me with a residency in Herzliya, Israel, where I was able to write much of this book. My colleagues there, Walter Zurko, Karni Eliasuf-Glusman, and the director of The Artists' Residency, Varda Genossar, were generous companions during my stay. For insight into aspects of Jewish culture and philosophy presented in the story, I'm particularly indebted to Rabbi Steven Greenberg, whose knowledge and passion have inspired me since we first met twenty-odd years ago. Though this is intended as a work of fiction, any misrepresentations of religious concepts remain entirely my own.

Naturalist and author Gerald Durrell, in his introduction to Franklin Russell's classic book *Watchers at the Pond* (1961), wrote: "Animals (yourself included) and plants are linked together like chains. Unfortunately, wherever you look, the weak link in the chain is man." This book is dedicated to Mimi Chenfeld and Mark Svede, two who strengthen the chain.

TABLE OF CONTENTS

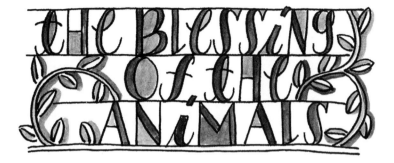

ARE DOGS JEWISH?

On the first day of fall, three weeks after school began, the summer heat barreled toward October as though it planned to steal another month for its season, and posters announcing the St. Francis Festival appeared on all the lightposts encircling the church across the street from Jared's apartment. That evening, Jared's friend Ian called up to the open third-floor window. Ian hadn't needed to shout; his always barking golden retriever, Bellow, had already heralded their arrival. Jared bounded down the wooden steps with Shayna, a yellow Lab who, for the last ten minutes, had been tossing her leash around in anticipation of their after-dinner walk. Beside Jared's driveway, Ian waited, ready to point out one of the posters.

"Remember, I was telling you about this?" Ian asked.

"I'm . . . not sure," Jared replied. He certainly knew about St. Francis—how could anyone not know about St. Francis? All his neighbors in the country even had figurines of the saint in their yards. But a St. Francis Festival? Jared hadn't known about that. He and his mother had only just moved to the neighborhood. Someone must have stapled up the posters while Jared had been working with his Hebrew tutor before dinner. In ten months Jared would turn thirteen, and he was rather behind in studying for his bar mitzvah. Changing neighborhoods three times in the last two years hadn't helped.

A neighbor revved up a blaring leafblower, so Jared and Ian and their dogs zipped across the street. Far enough away to be heard, Ian began again. "The Festival's the best part of going to St. Catherine's. It's a nice church and all, but the Festival's the coolest thing they do. Every year we go. I mean, Mom makes us go to Mass—you know, the Sunday-morning part. But the day before, we get the parade and the potluck and the blessing part. And the whole place is decorated with wild-bird feeders and streamers and posters and stuff. You'll see: everyone comes inside with their pets—like a hundred dogs and a hundred cats and hundreds of other animals, all kinds, and we all pack in together—not in the actual, you know, church part, with the pews and stained glass, but right inside the social hall."

While Bellow and Shayna sniffed out their own news at the lamppost, Jared studied the photocopied flyer of the bald man in a monk's robe: St. Francis of Assisi, patron saint of animals. A flock of creatures gazed up around him as he welcomed them with his wide-open arms. "That's two hundred dogs *and* cats? *Inside?* That's got to be all barking and yanking at leashes and hissing and scratching— No way, Ian. Cats don't even get along with cats, let alone dogs!"

"No, it's really, really peaceful. *Really.* I think the animals know they're in church and have to be quiet and behave."

"Oh, sure." Jared laughed. "They don't teach churchgoing in Shayna's obedience class and it's even Level Three! No, we'll come. Sounds great, but it doesn't sound peaceful."

The dogs suddenly jerked to attention, and Bellow veered off the sidewalk, towing Ian as he bounded toward a thick oak tree where a cocky squirrel chattered from the lowest limb. Bellow planted himself beside the trunk and commenced barking: *awruff* (pause) *awruff* (pause) *awruff* (pause) . . . as though he were giving the squirrel to the count of ten to climb down, or . . . or . . . or else! (It wasn't clear what else, since the squirrel had no intention of descending the tree.)

Eventually Ian managed to yank Bellow into a run and caught up with Jared and Shayna. "So anyway," Ian concluded, a little out of breath, "you have to come. You'll love it! Maybe Father Tim's blessing will even help Shayna win your next dog show."

"We'll be there," Jared said.

During their whole hour-long walk—across the wide lawn of St. Catherine's Church, which occupied the entire block; along streets with modest houses and streets with fancier houses where people scowled at the two friends even though they carried plastic bags for poop-scooping—Jared tried to imagine that motley flock of animals inside the church. Each time they passed a new poster, the image in his mind altered: first he pictured the blessing as a dog show, with everyone silent and Father Tim, like the kennel club judge, presiding in the center. Then Jared imagined something more like a circus: dogs and cats in separate rings, Father Tim as the ringmaster . . . Or like a petting zoo. Or a barnyard. Or Noah's ark. Or the Thanksgiving Day parade on TV, with St. Francis hovering like a giant float balloon over the spellbound crowd.

When Jared burst through the door at home, he immediately launched into a lengthy description of the Festival for his mother, as if, like Ian, he'd been attending it for years: ". . . and then there are goldfish and snakes, and it's like a pet store, except everyone's already bought the animals. And Ian says that the parade afterward is even more fun, because then the dogs don't have to just sit quiet and get blessed. And a potluck supper? Did I mention that? Mom? Mom—say something!"

"No, no. Don't let me interrupt your sermon," Jared's mother insisted. She'd bookmarked the page in the mystery she'd been reading and folded her hands on top of the paperback.

"Mom, I'm not giving a sermon. I'm just telling you how totally great the Festival is. Parents are invited, too."

"Oh, parents *and* pets. That's nice."

"Mom, quit it!"

"*And* Jews, too!" she added, smiling her pretend smile. "That's *extra* nice."

"Mother! What do you mean?"

"Have you completely, entirely, utterly, absolutely —or just accidentally?—overlooked the fact that—

hello?—we're Jewish? St. Francis may be part of Ian's faith, but not ours—"

"But still, I can take Shayna. She's *my* dog—and who says that *she's* Jewish?"

"Well, for starters, Shayna was your Hanukkah present—"

"But if I'm her owner, I should be able to decide what's okay for her. It's just a parade and, I don't know, I guess for one second inside Father Tim does a blessing or something."

"Or something. You don't even know what the heck it is you're invited to, Jared. What, is Shayna going to kneel for dog-biscuit Communion?"

"Mother!" Jared shouted, a little too loud for having a downstairs landlady.

When Jared argued with his mother, it was usually for permission to do something, or he would badger her to make an exception to one of her rules. Like most kids, Jared wished that his mother were more like other mothers; and like most mothers, she seemed to wish her son were less like other kids. But arguments were rarely about something having to do with religion.

Sometimes Jared could change his mother's mind by just wearing her out. He'd plead and remind her on the drive to school. Before bed. Waiting for pizza to be delivered. Walking to the bleachers, where his mother would wait while Jared took advanced obedience lessons with Shayna. And now, in the landlady's backyard, as his mother fanned the barely gray charcoal briquettes for their already late dinner, Jared began his latest campaign. Simply put, he intended to take their dog—*his* dog—to the annual Blessing of the Animals a week from that coming Saturday.

"Look, Mom, I read the entire poster again. It says '*Community* Festival' and '*Everyone* welcome.' It would say 'Christians only' if Jews weren't supposed to come."

Jared's mother squinted and spread her palms above the coals.

"You're blessing the charcoal?" Jared asked.

"Funny. Be a good kid and just pass me the spatula. Ready or not, burgers, it's show time!"

"Every single person I know gets to have their animals blessed. It's not fair. We live across the street! Shayna is—!"

"*Every single person*, is that right?" Jared's mother shut the lid of the grill with a sharp clunk, as though that might close the argument. "I *understand* that we're invited, Jared. But Jewish people don't worship St. Francis. Or St. *Anybody*. You know that. I also know you love Shayna and the other animals, but still—"

Jared took a moment to figure out what to say next. "So what do we have for blessing pets since we don't get St. Francis?"

"We? You mean we Jewish people?"

"No, I meant we Martians."

"Okay, okay, don't be a smart aleck. Frankly, I don't know if Jews have any special way of celebrating dogs or cats or . . ." This time Jared's mother paused to think, while Jared glared at her as though she were forgetting on purpose. "Succoth is kind of about nature and harvest, but that's not really animals, I guess. Maybe . . ."

Jared waited for an answer, though his mother seemed to be studying the temperature gauge on the grill. It read *Cool*. She rubbed a towel on its grimy dial, as if that might make the heat rise inside.

Finally Jared said, "So nothing about animals? We've got a blessing for candles, a blessing for bread—and there's even that Passover prayer about stupid *horse-radish*!—but what about something for pets that people love like—like part of the family?"

Jared's mother lifted her hands, palm sides up (one in an oven mitt), and shrugged her shoulders. "I'm not a Torah scholar. Maybe one of the great rabbis wrote about pets . . . but I've never heard . . ."

"It's not even inside the *holy* part of the church, it's just in the big room where they set up folding tables and chairs. And the parade goes right on the lawn, where I walk Shayna every—"

"That's not the point and you know it—"

"So everyone else gets to bring their dogs and cats

to the Festival, and all *I* get to do is sit in temple and listen to Rabbi Silver's speech about his latest trip to Jerusalem." Jared ducked under the picnic table to speak to Shayna, who'd been napping through the argument. "How about that, Shayna? Big whoop." The dog lifted her head and put it back down on her paws. She never had anything to add when the talk overhead had that bickering tone.

"Now you're sounding disrespectful. I'm willing to discuss this with my son, but not with some wisecracker. The priest is not going to include Shayna in his St. Francis Day blessing. We are Jewish. That is final."

"But *Shayna's* not Jewish! It's not like she takes bat mitzvah lessons or goes to temple or believes in anything except—except *cheese*! . . . and dog biscuits . . . and other dogs . . . and me and you. In that order. Right, Shayna?" Jared held open his arms to the dog and Shayna inched over for a hug. "And what about Bellow? He likes bagels—and Ian's family's *Catholic*."

A wisp of smoke snaked from the grill as Jared's

mother lifted its lid. "And how, smart guy, just how do you know that Shayna's not Jewish?" His mother poked at the pink patties and flattened them, hoping they'd cook faster. "Maybe if a dog belongs to a Jewish family, then the dog becomes Jewish, kind of like this home is a Jewish home, even though we're only renting the top floor from Mrs. Lewison and she isn't Jewish. Well, most of the folks in the neighborhood aren't. Anyway, I think I made a good point, and I want you to think about that. Will you?"

"You need a before-dinner walk, Shaynalayna? You do? Let's go," Jared decided for the dog.

"I just asked you to think about something."

"I can do two things at once."

Jared's mother pulled off the oven mitt and walked over to take her son's shoulders. "This is a complicated question, I admit it."

"It's only complicated because you won't let me," Jared stated, the meanness in his voice camouflaging the crack that crying might have made.

"But asking questions is a pretty Jewish thing. A

good thing. Remember at Passover, the Four Questions? Remember how the different rabbis all have different answers? Maybe we should do the same thing about this St. Francis business," she proposed, her words sounding more enthusiastic as she pursued her new suggestion. "Let's ask some people about our being Jewish and taking Shayna to this Catholic ceremony and see what opinions we can find."

"So, what if everyone thinks it's okay to go—are you going to let me?"

"And . . . what if everyone says it's *not* okay? Are you going to be upset? Let's just ask and see what we find out. You talk with people this weekend. At Sunday school, for instance. And I'll do some inquiring myself."

Jared clipped on Shayna's leash and shrugged a yes answer.

"Deal? I'd like more than a shrug."

"All right, yes."

"Thank you. So will you try for, say, four opinions? And I'll also get four. And I promise I won't make the decision for you. You'll decide." Then Jared's mother held out her hand for an official shake on it. Jared obliged her.

"Ready? Shayna? You give us the first opinion. Want to go? *Want to go?*" he asked, his voice rising with excitement at the end of the phrase just as the obedience instructor had taught him.

Shayna, of course, yipped an unambiguous *yes*.

"All right, Shayna! All right!" Jared smiled back at his mother. "Don't worry, Mom. I won't count Shayna as one of my four."

"But I'm counting on you for dinner," she called. "Be back in fifteen minutes. Not that these burgers will be cooked before sunrise . . ."

# FRANCIS WITHOUT THE "SAINT PART"

St. Francis of Assisi had posed a problem for Jared's family long before Jared had ever heard of the Blessing of the Animals. Two years earlier, Jared had set his heart on having a statue of St. Francis for their yard. This happened around the time his parents separated, when the three of them still shared the renovated farmhouse at the orchard where his father still lived and worked. In that small town, where most of the people have acres and acres and sometimes even *more* acres of land, a statue of St. Francis presides in most yards. Reaching out with open arms, he's usually surrounded by deer, squirrels, rabbits, raccoons, or other woodland creatures—all of them cast from clay or concrete. At the nearby pottery outlets, whole crowds of animals line the highway like different bands or lodge chapters in a parade: squirrels and rabbits, geese and swans, and a long assembly of tall St. Francises: the tallest ones bless the medium-size St. Francises, and those saints pray over even smaller and smaller versions. It looks as if the same saint has been planted at different times throughout the growing season.

Jared used to wonder why his country neighbors would want statues of the very animals—the deer, squirrels, Canada geese—that in real life often wandered from the woods or glided from the sky right onto their lawns. Some animals, like rabbits and raccoons, many of their neighbors would even try to shoot if a real one so much as tiptoed across their grass. But Jared loved to find those creatures on his family's land. He'd already posted a dozen bird feeders that he'd built with his great-grandfather. Especially before the school bus arrived, Jared toured the or-

chard's trails and meadows without Shayna, whose presence tended to scare any other creature they'd meet.

But a St. Francis for their yard? "Out of the question," his parents declared, pouncing on the exact same words at nearly the exact same moment. (Although his parents often talked at the same time, they rarely shared the same idea, it seemed, even then.) How could a Jewish family have a sculpture of St. Francis? his parents asked. Well, they couldn't. And Jared's mother had told him so repeatedly, despite the fact that, once in a while, she used to call him "Francis," without the "Saint" part, since animals were as interested in Jared as he was in them.

As a toddler, Jared preferred his father's field guides to children's books. Every sunny weekend day he wanted to go to the zoo, or to the park where all the nature trails are labeled, or to any county fair where people bring livestock to be judged. When he was four, a giraffe leaned its neck as close to the fence as it could, directly in front of Jared, just to sniff him. No one else. Not only squirrels but seven-stripe chipmunks would eat Frosty O's from Jared's open hand. All three indoor cats used to come to Jared when he called. (The cats still lived with his father because Mrs. Lewison would not permit four pets in the new apartment. But the cats didn't come for his father.) And as for Shayna, which means "beautiful" in Yiddish, his great-grandfather's language, she and Jared might as well have shared the same name. When his mother called Jared, the dog automatically came, too. And when she called Shayna, Jared naturally went along to see what his mother could want with her.

"But really, why do you want a St. Francis statue?" his mother had wondered.

"Just because he loved animals, the way I do," Jared had explained. "He's the king of animal lovers. It's not like I want a Mary statue or a cross or anything. And Ms. Connors at school says that even if you don't believe in him, all the animals know they're safe and welcome in the yard when they see you've got a St. Francis."

"Hmm. If Ms. Connors was your zoology teacher

instead of your art teacher, I might be more persuaded . . . but regardless, Jared, we don't have a Christmas tree, right?—even though we think they're beautiful."

"But we get Hanukkah," Jared had replied, "so we don't need Christmas."

"Honey, not that argument! We've been through this: Christmas and Hanukkah have nothing in common. They happen around the same time, period. Like Easter and Passover: completely different, but nearby—"

"All I know is, we get gypped out of a lot of stuff."

Although it had nothing to do with St. Francis, as it so happened, the day after that discussion Jared and his mother began packing. Her application to rent an apartment half an hour away in the city had been accepted. Since they would now be without a yard—let alone woods and acres of wildlife—the St. Francis topic had been dropped.

On his way to school the morning after first discussing the Festival, Jared took his usual shortcut across St.

Catherine's lawn. He was heading through the mostly empty parking lot, intending to continue straight down East Hardwick Street, when suddenly a flurry of paper slid across the asphalt toward him. A man balancing an armload of boxes had dropped one of his packages. Jared leaped to retrieve the papers blowing his way—they turned out to be more Festival posters—and worked toward the church entrance, collecting the strewn pages, until he came alongside the man just resting the upended box on the hood of a car.

As Jared tucked the collected posters back into the opened box, he realized it was Father Tim who had dropped them.

"Thank you, thank you. I always try to carry too many things at once," Father Tim said. "It's not as if I can't make two trips!" The priest folded down the lid on the open box and extended his hand. "Now, I know you, don't I? You're in my . . ."

"I don't think so," Jared said. "But I know you're Father Tim."

"Yes. And your name, my friend?"

"It's Jared," he replied, shaking the priest's hand. "But maybe, since I live right across the street—that house right over there—you might recognize me. I'm the kid who's always walking a dog here."

"Oh yes? What kind of dog?"

"A yellow Lab—" Jared reached into his windbreaker pocket and produced an empty sandwich bag. "But I always clean up after her, so I don't leave her messes on your lawn."

"That's good of you, Jared. We're having a whole kennel's worth of dogs for the Festival. I'll make a note to pick up a few boxes of sandwich bags, just to have around." Father Tim lifted up one of the Festival posters and pointed to the date as if Jared hadn't noticed the printed side. "I hope you'll be bringing your Lab to the Blessing. Did you say a 'yellow Lab'? I used to have a chocolate Lab until last year. Lost her at fourteen. Pretty long life for a Lab. Anyway, the more animals the merrier."

"Um, I'd like to, we'd all like to come. I mean, my mom might not, but we might. I'm not sure if—"

Jared didn't want to lie to the priest, but then he didn't know what would be worse: saying that he was coming and then not showing up, or saying that he wasn't coming. Both answers sounded insulting. Or maybe, Jared thought, maybe I should just tell Father Tim I'm Jewish and see what he says.

Father Tim rescued Jared before he could decide. "Well, just know that you're welcome. Our St. Francis Festival attracts people from all over the city. It's our big day for families and children—and, of course, animals."

"Can I ask you one question about it?" Briefly Jared wondered if maybe Father Tim's opinion could be one of the four he needed to seek.

The priest picked up two of his boxes again. "Sure can. That is, if you'll open the church door for me."

Jared blocked the open door with his body and Father Tim entered the vestibule. On the other hand, Jared realized, a priest probably wasn't the right person to help solve a Jewish person's predicament. "I just wondered," Jared asked, "what actually happens during the blessing part? See, I've never been to it before, though my friend Ian Flint, he always comes and says it's great."

"Oh, Ian Flint. I've known Ian and his family for years. I—well, you didn't ask about the Flints. Let's see. Basically, I recite a few prayers . . . Now, I take it you do know a little about St. Francis . . ."

"Oh, right, a lot. Not a lot, but I know about how he cared for animals and how he's the patron saint of animals."

"Correct. And so the congregation joins me in a couple of short prayers—I try to keep things short, since it's pretty crowded with everyone and everyone's pets in the building. I usually offer a mini-sermon about the richness of creation and the piety of this amazingly devoted man who lived and preached a life of complete poverty and discipline for Christ. Then I wrap up with a benediction and sprinkle holy water upon the assembly, blessing every creature in the name of the Father, Son, and Holy Spirit."

"You put holy water on every single animal? And

the people, too?" Jared's heart sank as he thought of the priest drawing a cross over Shayna's face and reciting words like "Jesus Christ" right over his own head.

"Oh, of course not! That would take all day. No, I just cast the water above the crowd. I have a special—well, it's like a wand, I suppose, that helps send the droplets from the altar. And if we manage to leave any aisles at all, I try to go into the room and perform the anointing here and there, just a few places, so people can feel closer to the ceremony." Jared followed Father Tim outdoors again, where the priest lifted the last two boxes from his car.

"So, if I were in the audience with my dog, Shayna, we'd get the blessing even if you didn't put the holy water right on her . . ."

"It's more the idea of just being there than actually feeling the holy water. But yes, the whole room receives the blessing. That's the beauty of it. And of course, you'll like the parade and the potluck—our congregation specializes in desserts, it seems!"

Behind Father Tim, a group of kids from Jared's

school walked past. "Father Tim," Jared said, "I don't mean to be rude, but I just realized if I don't hurry I'll be late for school."

"Oh, of course. I shouldn't have held you up—"

"But thank you for explaining it all." Jared saw that Father Tim had extended his hand again, and shook it quickly.

"That's what I'm here for. And next time you're walking your dog, knock on my window. It's the first one by the door here. You'll recognize me inside. There's even a picture of Standish—he was my Lab— on the sill."

Jared's father picked him up Friday after school for their usual every-other-weekend visit. They'd do some apple picking, which Jared felt was sort of half-chore, half-fun, maybe make cider, and certainly grill something for supper. (His father even grilled in the dead of winter; it was the only cooking he really enjoyed.) In the early morning, they'd set out with a group of bird-watchers Jared had met through his old Scout troop. Among other things, someone had learned the location of a great horned owl's nest. Jared's life list of birds included 118 species to date; that owl would be a new addition.

Jared's parents' separation was only a trial, they had explained. They weren't officially divorced, and at least they both *said* that they hoped a year apart would bring them back together. Unfortunately, that was two years ago; fortunately, his mother continued to sign only month-to-month leases with their landlady. His parents did spend some time together—mostly talking with their marriage counselor or overlapping for a meal as they passed Jared from one home to the other. All Jared could do was add his own hope.

He could force himself to imagine his parents remarried or divorced—he'd begun to wonder if there could be much difference any longer between being separated and being divorced. And he could imagine stepbrothers or stepsisters, too. But Jared couldn't bear the idea that, in addition to whatever his parents might do, he'd have to live in the city forever, without his own yard and with only one

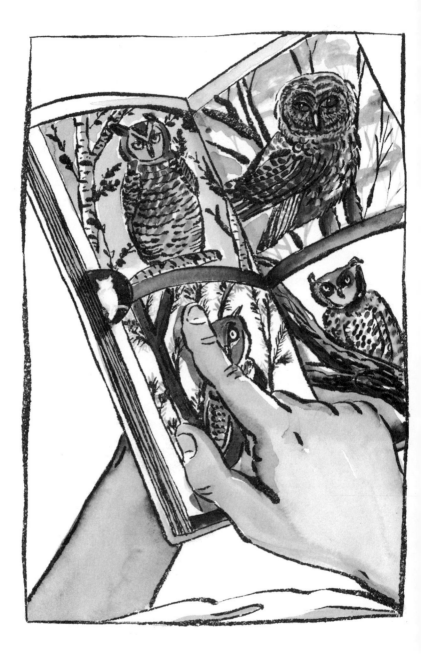

pet—giving up the life he'd so loved among their acres at the orchard.

Even before he and his father arrived at the gates and the long grove of apple and peach trees that wended toward the house, Jared brought up the St. Francis Festival. Though he knew his father's permission was probably the last thing that might change his mother's opinion, he had to ask. It was part of the deal, the research. So Jared explained about the blessing and Shayna and the conversations he'd had of late. "So, like on Passover—you know, we read how the different rabbis have different interpretations—well, I'm supposed to collect four people's thoughts."

His father said, "Good plan," and then he either didn't know what answer to give or had to focus on the winding road with the small hills that, if he took them too quickly, sent a wave of dizziness up Jared's neck. Finally his father nodded his head in agreement. "This time, I'm going along with your mom: a priest's prayers are for his congregation; a rabbi's prayers are for his."

"Why does everyone keep saying things like that? It's not true! Remember, we all went to Tina-next-door's wedding? And we all went to the funeral of that lady I didn't even really know, right at St. Catherine's—all of us did, and Father Tim blessed everybody there, remember? He didn't say, 'Okay, all you Jewish people, be sure and duck now so that my blessing doesn't touch you.' "

"Very funny, mister." Jared's father's laughter started Jared laughing, though he meant to keep a serious face. "But we all went to Tina's wedding out of love and respect for our friends. I don't know if it's fair to compare the two—but I do see your point."

"You do?" Jared wasn't sure, but maybe he should have mentioned speaking with Father Tim earlier in the week—the part about the holy water and the sign of the cross, which was still less than clear to him.

"Sure, I see your point. It's a fair point. I'm not sure I see it the way you see it, since no one at St. Catherine's would be hurt—the way our friends who got married would be hurt—if you missed this St. Francis event. But to be fair, I'd say fine, take Shayna if it honestly means that much to you."

"Yes! Yes! It's one for Shayna!" Jared shouted, surprising himself at how happy his father's answer made him.

"But that's only *my* opinion," his father added, pushing the garage door opener above the visor. "That's just *one* opinion. You need three more, right? But . . . if you do end up going, just remember: *Duck!*"

On Saturday, the Festival was not mentioned even once during the bird-watching trip. Jared and his father stopped for lunch afterward with Pappap and Grams, Jared's ninety-two-year-old great-grandparents, who lived very close to the orchard. After the meal, while his father made tea and helped Grams fill out some insurance forms, Jared sanded wooden bat houses with Pappap in the workshop that used to be the garage when Pappap drove. Jared and his father had already nailed dozens of the bat houses they'd constructed all around the orchards and the main house—it was hard to tell if attracting bats really helped with the mosquito problem or not.

Jared didn't know if Pappap would be a good person to ask. He didn't want any of his four opinions to be "No." He had considered asking only people who were sure bets for a "yes" answer—people like Ian, or the groundskeeper at St. Catherine's, who always carried a treat for Shayna, or Jared's dog training instructor, who'd probably say the Festival was a perfect chance to socialize Shayna for the upcoming meet. But Jared knew his mother wouldn't consider those legitimate opinions.

"Pappap, Mom and I are having a fight."

"A fight?"

"I mean, a discussion."

"Oh. Well, you know what Pappap says: Great-grandchildren are always right. But just the same, what's the topic?"

"Well, I want to take Shayna to the Blessing of the Animals across the street at St. Catherine's Church.

Remember, there's this special saint,  St. Francis, who blessed the animals?"

"Yes, I know something of him. Go on."

"Well, this one day all the animals in the neighborhood get to come inside the church and be blessed. So the question is, don't you think Shayna can go, since, really, *she* isn't the one who's Jewish."

"I see." Pappap fished in his jacket for a moment, producing the pocketknife that Jared had loved as a baby. Pappap never went anywhere without it, and Jared always used to reach into his pocket to find it. He hadn't known it was a knife. It was simply something too heavy for its little size, with smooth and wrinkled wood that felt good in his small hand.

Pappap whittled at the splintered edge of a board. "In the old country, in the Russian village where I grew up and your first great-grandma you never knew—may she rest in peace—where she grew up, no one owned dogs. Dogs were strays—wild, like rats. They were with the alley cats. Garbage eaters. No one named them or thought of them as pets. We never hurt them, since they were God's creatures, but to be friends? No, we didn't know dogs could be beautiful and smart and loving like Shayna."

Jared turned and covered his ears while Pappap switched on his handsaw to make another cut in a sheet of poplar. Pappap's hands, even at ninety-two, remained powerful and steady. At the holidays, when the whole family assembled, the same contest was waged: No one there—not his son or daughter, not one of his three grandsons and two granddaughters, not his one great-grandson, Jared, no wife or current boyfriend or dinner guest—no one could beat Pappap at arm wrestling.

Pappap had worked almost full-time until he turned seventy-eight. He'd owned a business that recycled tires, and for most of those years, he heaved around car tires and even truck tires that could weigh more than a hundred pounds apiece. Though Jared's father tried to convince his grandfather to give up using power drills and saws, Pappap would concede only two things: driving, because he'd had a few fender-benders and near-misses—either his eyes or his reaction time failed him—and long periods of standing, because his back didn't like to lean for hours at the workbench. So now Pappap sat and hammered and sawed and drilled from the first light of day until lunchtime, and sometimes all afternoon as well.

Once the roaring blade whined down to a halt, Pappap began exactly where he had left off, though Jared had wondered if Pappap had forgotten the question.

"Jared, I know you love animals. I love them, too. But I'm wondering, is your problem really about the dog? I'm wondering, what's so important about this blessing day? Do you think Shayna will miss being there?"

"No, but *I* will! Do *I* have to be the only kid in the whole neighborhood who isn't going? I mean, there's me and the three Markus girls and Allan Horvath (whose mom, I guess, is Jewish)—*total*! We're the only Jewish kids in the whole school."

"But what about at shul?"

"That's half an hour away. The kids there, I mean they're friends, but not my everyday friends."

Jared passed his great-grandfather the bat house he'd been sanding, and Pappap smoothed the wood with his huge hands, inspecting each surface.

"Use maybe a little more of the Very Fine on the roof? But me, if I were a bat, I'd want to live in one of your houses." Pappap handed back the box. "So, my Jared, is it you just don't want to be different? Where we live, where you live—where most people live in America—Jewish is different, I know. Maybe some places it's not so different, but here . . ."

"That's not the only reason." Jared scrubbed and scrubbed with the sandpaper. He could already see Pappap's answer coming. What was the point of continuing their talk? He wanted to put down the bat house and wait in the car.

"You know, I forget about being a little boy—I mean a *not-so-little* boy. It's . . . it's eighty years ago I was your age. I forget what it was like, I know. And I lived among many Jewish families, so we were not so different then, in Europe. Different started when I came to this country. I had no English, true, but also we went from having enough money and a nice place to live and friends and jobs to having not so much of any of that. We were different in every way, and it was hard, and it took too many years of struggling—we had many days of tears and worries and troubles. Eventually, though, we found we could be proud of who we were, which wasn't just like our neighbors. We could be a little proud of knowing three languages—Yiddish and Russian and now English. Proud of our history. So after a while, it grew to be a nice feeling not to do everything just like everyone around us."

Jared couldn't remember Pappap saying so many sentences at once. Generally Pappap let Grams do most of the talking. But now, recalling more of his first years in this new country, Pappap showed no sign of stopping, not even when Jared's father shouted from the back door that it was time to shove off. Jared guessed that his great-grandfather hadn't heard the faraway summons and interrupted: "Pappap, I understand what you're saying about settling in America and all that. But in my case, what would you do? What's your opinion about me taking Shayna to the Festival?"

"I was taking the long way to tell you, wasn't I? I should have taken a shortcut. But I say this: Be proud you are Jewish in that neighborhood of yours, and no, stay home with the dog. I wish that you'll stay home, but only to show yourself how glad you can feel just for being the person you are—not the same person as everybody—to show how proud you are for being a Jew."

"Okay, well, whatever. I need to go now, Dad's calling me." Jared stood and looked at the dust on the floor, at the whittled curls of wood—at anything but Pappap's eyes. "I figured you'd say I shouldn't be allowed to go."

"Then, young man, you misunderstood me. I did not say you shouldn't be allowed." Pappap restated his words slowly: "I said . . . I wished . . . you would . . . all by yourself . . . decide not to go . . . and to be happy about that."

Jared's father called again. Jared shouted, "Coming! Coming!" brushed the wood dust from his shorts, and leaned to kiss Pappap's scratchy cheek. "I understand. Thanks, Pappap. See you next week, maybe. Love you."

Racing back to the car, Jared didn't know what to think. He didn't want to agree with his great-grandfather, but what Pappap had said sounded partly right. There was something good about being different. No one else in school trained dogs. No one else used to live in an apple orchard.

Two opinions down. Two to go. So far, so good? Jared wasn't sure.

# A PART OF THE PLAN

At Sunday school, Jared's class punched nail-hole patterns in Band-Aids tins. They were crafting scent boxes to be used for celebrating Havdalah and the sweetness of Sabbath's end. Like most Sunday-school projects, it would come home with Jared, his mother would say how beautiful it was, and then she'd store it in a drawer. No, they didn't always keep the Sabbath. Sometimes Jared wished his family would—that they'd enjoy being Jewish more, instead of just going to temple and preparing for his bar mitzvah—but most of the time Jared prayed simply that his family would be together, all three of them, again. At temple or any-where else.

For his next opinion, Jared decided to pose his dilemma to his teacher Mr. Goldfarb, who knew six languages (unfortunately, English worst of all). He was a retired translator who had come to America as a teenager, a refugee from the camps of the Holocaust. When Jared's class studied World War II, Mr. Goldfarb had rolled up the long-sleeve white shirt he always wore and let the students touch the tattooed numbers on his skin. Though he wasn't mean, or even strict with the class, Mr. Goldfarb didn't always say things the nicest way in English.

And one more thing about his teacher: Twenty years earlier, Jared's mother had been in Mr. Gold-farb's same Sunday-school class. (Apparently his English was much worse then.) If Mr. Goldfarb said yes, his mother would *have* to let Shayna go to the blessing on Saturday.

After class, Jared explained the situation and posed his question. "Could I take my dog to the St. Francis

Festival, since dogs don't really have a religion like Jewish—or do they?—and . . ."

"No, you've found a bad question. Never are dogs Jewish. No!" Mr. Goldfarb shook his head as though Jared exasperated him every single week, which was hardly the case. "It is no good to use the word 'dog' with the word 'Jew.' In concentration camps, the Nazis called us 'Jewish dogs.' *Jewish dogs*. They spit out worst names yet. We were despised with more cruelty treatment than even a real dog should suffer."

Jared remained silent for a moment, trying to show respect. "I know that was terrible." He stopped again, momentarily thinking that Mr. Goldfarb might change the subject back for him. Jared watched his teacher place check marks in his attendance notebook. Finally, he said, "But I don't understand, Mr. Goldfarb. Does that mean if a person who's Jewish has a dog and he—"

"What already I have said, Jared, is a dog is a dog. And they can be nice, dogs. My wife—we have a dog, even, a little mixed-up kind . . . How do you call them?

A peek-a-poo. But my ears cannot listen to the word 'dog' next to 'Jew' without thinking hateful people. You see, I am the wrong person to ask, perhaps. Let's together go and find our Rabbi Silver to ask."

"So, in your opinion, I really shouldn't—"

"In my opinion, a Jew would never ask such a question. But you are asking. Fine. Come, our rabbi will have an answer."

Heading toward the synagogue office, Jared had a horrible picture in his mind. All he could think of was Shayna left out of the blessing: all the pets in the whole city celebrating inside St. Catherine's Church, except for Shayna. Jared could see her outside Father Tim's window in the pouring-down rain. Everyone inside had called her a Jewish dog, just like Mr. Goldfarb told him. And everyone hated her and banished her from their company. I have to get the rabbi's permission, Jared thought to himself. He has to has to has to say yes.

While Rabbi Silver had an office, he mostly liked to walk and talk. Fast walking. Fast talking. Mr. Goldfarb nabbed the rabbi just as he passed the preschool wing, introduced Jared's question briefly, and then handed off his student to the rabbi as though Jared were a baton in a relay race. Rabbi Silver patted Jared on the back to start the pace, and took off on another lap around the synagogue hallways.

Just thirty years old, recently married, and only a year in town, Rabbi Silver had succeeded the congregation's original rabbi. Rabbi Blonder had married Grandma and Grandpa, who lived in the area until moving south a few years ago, as well as Jared's mother and father.

Rabbi Silver had a yarmulke collection. He bobby-pinned a different one in his thick hair every day (Jared couldn't recall seeing the same one twice), so that it wouldn't blow off as he rushed around the building. (Jared's always did.) Whenever someone in the congregation went to Israel—or anywhere embroidered or knitted or quilted yarmulkes can be found—the rabbi received a yarmulke as a present. That morning, gold threads wove grapevines around his cap, and purple beads made clusters for the grapes. Jared had simply borrowed one of the black yarmulkes stock-piled in the wooden box by the temple door.

"Rabbi, what do you think? I have three opinions so far—sort of—and I promised my mom that I'd get four. She's finding four—"

"Tell me again the question in your own words. Firsthand's always better."

"Well, sure. I just want to know if it's a sin or any-thing if I take Shayna (she's my dog) to the St. Francis Festival at St. Catherine's. This one day, Father Tim does his blessing over the animals—and there's a pa-rade and a potluck supper. Since, well, since I'm Jew-ish, what about my dog? My family's even been to St. Catherine's before. For a funeral once, and a wedding, too. And I walk our dog there all the time."

"I see. This isn't a question I'm asked every day. Let me think a moment." Rabbi Silver strode through the hallways, not really peering into the classrooms, not really looking out the windows into the courtyard. Jared matched his pace.

"Hmm. Let me assure you of one thing first: It's fine for you and your family to join in a celebration with friends at their church, to share in a friend's loss at a different place of worship, to be a Jew honoring another person's beliefs. That's being compassionate, a good quality to have. That's the easy part of my answer."

"I guess I understand that part. What about the harder part?"

Rabbi Silver sighed and began again, speaking more deliberately this time. "Now, first of all, a dog cannot be Jewish. No animal can. It's that simple. Because, to be a Jew, you have to make a promise with God. We call that a covenant, and it just means you make a contract with the Almighty. A commitment to Him. Dogs cannot do that. Even a pretty smart dog, which I gather you have."

"Yes, I mean, no. I mean, Shayna's really smart, but she couldn't do that contract thing with God."

"That's right. But, more importantly, all animals *are already part* of God's natural world, a part of His will, a part of the beauty God wanted in the world. So they don't need to make this contract, lucky dogs." The rabbi paused a moment to open the double doors in the lobby. "Ah, but people . . . we're different. God created each human animal with a mind of its own. You and I—we have our own independent, strong wills—know what I mean?"

"Sure. Mom sometimes says I'm too strong-willed—because, because I guess I don't always want to do just what she says. But she's got the same strong will, because she almost never wants to do what *I* say."

"No, we all are strong-willed to some degree, parents especially. That's their job. But let's leave that topic for another walk. So, Jared, unlike the animals, each human being has to say yes, I want to be a Jew, I want to make a promise with God. And we need to renew that promise every day. Still with me?"

"Sure, so far. But maybe you could walk a little slower."

"Of course, sorry. My only exercise." The rabbi stopped beside the temple gift shop to complete his explanation. "You see, your dog—it's Shayna, right?" Jared nodded his head. "Shayna simply doesn't need a priest's blessing. She doesn't need a rabbi's either, because a dog is always a perfect part of God's plan, just the way it is."

"So, Rabbi, um, if I took Shayna over for Father Tim's blessing, there would be, like, no reason, because dogs are already blessed?"

"Right . . . and not only is your Shayna in harmony with God's wonderful creation, but also your life blesses Shayna. All your kindnesses, all the care you give her, and every way you're gentle and good to your dog—all these are a kind of prayer. And what's more, by your caring for Shayna, she has helped you to understand the power of kindness, which is also part of God's will. She helps you fulfill your promise to God. See?"

Jared knew the rabbi was waiting for him to reply as he commenced walking again down the corridor, this time more slowly. Probably his father's car was also waiting in the parking lot. But Jared hardly knew what to say. He'd never thought that caring for animals had anything to do with God or with being Jewish. Rabbi Silver wasn't telling him to go or not to go. Attending the St. Francis Festival suddenly wasn't the point at all. Jared's mind froze, or stumbled, or something, because now he couldn't think of how to respond. This fourth opinion blurred everything.

"Rabbi," Jared stuttered, "I bet my dad's waiting outside, but I sort of understand what you were saying. So, when I'm walking or training or playing with Shayna, I just have to remember, that's kind of like a thank-you-God prayer?"

Rabbi Silver stopped as though they'd reached the finish line. Coincidentally, they had reached the main entrance doors. "That's a good way to think of it. You get to be your own St. Francis. But a Jewish version, without the shaved head and the halo." Rabbi Silver pointed to the top of his head.

"Thanks again," Jared replied, and pushed his back against the large wooden doors to leave the temple.

"Your yarmulke?" the rabbi called.

"Oh, right!" Jared slapped the top of his head, slid off the borrowed yarmulke, and dunked it back into the box. He'd been meaning to gather up all the ones he'd accidentally worn home (glove compartments, backpack, phone drawer, coat pockets) and return them to the temple. Next week, he promised himself.

# EIGHT
## ANSWERS

Jared's father dropped him off at school early Monday after their three nights together, and his mother picked him up after school. Shayna sometimes joined Jared for his weekend in the country, but this weekend she'd stayed home and kept his mother company. Today, his mother had brought the dog along, and Shayna's head craned from the passenger-seat window, watching for Jared.

"Hey! Shaynalayna! Hey, Mom!" Jared called through the open windows. The trunk popped up, and Jared tossed his backpack inside and wedged a half-full bushel basket of Cortland apples beside it (he'd passed out the other half at school). Then he jumped into the front seat and tugged the exuberant dog onto his lap so he could close the door.

"I figured we might give Shayna an extra-special walk along the lake," said his mother, *"just in case* she doesn't get to be in the parade Saturday. You know, a consolation prize."

"Thanks," Jared said, "that's nice, Mom. I don't have much homework anyway. Just stupid geometry."

"Geometry can't be stupid, but people who don't study their geometry can be." His mother smiled.

Amazingly, they drove for ten minutes and talked only about what each had done over the weekend. Jared's mother had wallpapered her bedroom—it took twice as long as she'd planned, and Mrs. Lewison liked it so much she offered to pay for the paper. His mother had gone to a movie with a friend—no, not a special friend, just a friend friend. Jared, meantime, took out his field guide and pointed to the new birds he'd added to his life list: "So, besides the great horned owl, which did not move the whole time we were there—it just slept way up in a tree—we spotted a whole flock of cedar waxwings: really cool birds with, you know, kind of a Mohawk haircut."

At the lake, his mother parked near a small marina where people tended to feed the ducks, so there were usually some for Shayna to chase. As they climbed the crumbling stones toward the water, both Jared and his mother wondered who would bring up the Festival first.

"Okay, sonny boy," his mother said abruptly, heaving a stick for Shayna as far as she could into the water. "I found four opinions."

"I found four, too," Jared answered.

"Good. So . . . ? Do you think we should share them now?"

Jared stared at his mother. He couldn't believe she was being so cool. "No, Mom, how about if we share them *after* the Festival, so I could just take Shayna and then we'd find out?"

That was worth laughing about. Jared's mother

pretended to bonk Jared on the noggin with her fist, Jared ducked, and they raced a few yards down the beach, dodging each other, until his mother gave up. "Enough, enough," she announced, and took a quick deep breath. "Here's my report. I called your Aunt Cynthia in Manhattan, who sends you her love, first of all—"

"Shoot! *I* should have called her. I could have talked to Jeremy."

"Well, you could have. But Aunt Cynthy tells me that at Jeremy's school every child celebrates everything, since there's such a melting pot of faiths there. They experience a few Jewish and a few Christian holidays at school, and they also give up certain foods during lunch to honor Muslim Ramadan. They share in Chinese New Year, and in the Buddhist Water Festival, which is your cousin Jeremy's favorite, since the whole class has a water fight in the parking lot with hoses and water balloons and giant squirt guns."

"That'd be awesome! How come we can't live across the street from a Buddhist temple?"

"As I was saying"—Jared's mother continued, her sneakers balancing on the flat stones that dotted the bubbly margin of surf—"Aunt Cynthy says it's a wonderful educational opportunity. She's also convinced that every child knows which religion is his or hers and which are the other children's—so that's not a problem. So she'd give you *her* blessing to go the St. Francis blessing."

"Okay, so one for us, Shayna!" Jared grabbed the stick from the returning wet dog's jaws and hurled it.

"Excuse me, this isn't supposed to be a vote. We're not tallying the number of fors and againsts."

"Sorry—I was just"—Jared made a quick substitution—"just excited to hear that you talked to Aunt Cynthy. It's funny, it was kind of hard to tell from the people I talked to who was for and who was against my going." Jared jumped a few feet ahead, did an about-face, and walked backward in front of his mother, watching his footprints trail back toward the car.

"Well, hard question, hard answers. Meanwhile, for

my second opinion . . . drum roll . . . I talked to Cantor Bloom at our temple."

"Sheeze-o-peeze! Why him? Let me guess," Jared said. "He said forget it."

"No . . . let me *tell you*, instead. He explained to me how the Jewish teachings don't really have good things to say about dogs. *Or* cats. They're thought of only as strays and vermin in the Torah. No one had pets the way we do today."

"That's kind of what Pappap said."

"Really? Well, they're close to the same age, maybe grew up in similar communities in the old country. But the cantor says our idea of animal companionship—not just working animals or livestock—is so new that the great sages never really wrote about it. Finally, he arrived at a conclusion after rambling on for a while about a variety of things, including wolves and llamas and unicorns—"

"Unicorns! Llamas? No way!"

"I added that myself. Just wishing you'd lighten up, honey. But then—and I know you won't like to hear this part—then he said, on the other hand, the Torah does talk a lot about parents and how a parent's word must be respected."

"Yeah, yeah, the honor-thy-mother-and-father stuff. What about a new eleventh commandment: 'Thou shalt respect thy son's opinion every now and then.' " It was easier for Jared to look at his mother's footprints than at her face. His feet were going one way and hers were coming the opposite way. Sometimes she planted a foot directly over his footprint, as though she was trying to change his direction, or maybe meet him halfway.

"Well, I'd say the cantor's opinion is more like a pass—that is, if we were voting, and we're not. I just appreciated his thoughts: I never stopped to think that having dogs and cats as family members wasn't something most people did hundreds and hundreds of years ago when the Torah was being written."

"I guess I didn't either. But you'd still think—well, I don't know. So that's two. Two more. Who else? Who else?"

"I called the Markus family, but they must be out of town. I just wondered if their kids were going. But I did reach Mrs. Horvath, who said she'd never heard of St. Francis's—"

"She hasn't heard of St. Francis? Come on!" Jared threw up his arms in amazement. "Has she heard of St. Louis? I mean, she had to have seen the posters?"

"You are one funny boy, Jared. If you would let me finish: Mrs. Horvath hadn't heard of St. Francis's blessing as part of a church service. But she did understand our issue—at first, anyway—but then she ended up telling me a long story about when she was bitten by this German shepherd dog as a little girl and how she's very frightened of dogs, even today, and on and on and on."

"Must run in the family. Sounds like Allan, too. He takes forever to say things in class."

"But she did say this, which I thought was sensible. She said, History proves that Jews will disappear if there's nothing to distinguish us from our neighbors."

"I know that. In current events Mr. Goldfarb talks

about how the number of Jews keeps decreasing in the world." Jared stooped to gather a handful of shale, perfect for skipping, and flung the first piece across the water. "Eight skips!"

"Anyway, Mrs. Horvath feels that just living in America automatically teaches a person—every person—the Christian traditions. They wash over you. Like a flood. You don't have to even try to learn Christian ideas and holidays. But for Jewish things, you have to go and find that information."

Jared launched another and another stone across the surface. Eleven skips. Four skips. "What's that mean?"

"I mean, if you don't seek out Judaism, you won't get it just by living here, every day, melting in the American melting pot. You have to—I don't know. You have to go to the well of Jewish learning and lower your bucket and haul it up to the top and start drinking!" Jared's mother laughed at her own silly metaphor.

"That makes it real clear, Mom," Jared replied as he fired another round of shale at the water.

"You know what I mean. Actually, I liked talking with Allan's mother."

"Mom, wait one second. Let me call Shayna," Jared interrupted, and whistled to bring the dog closer.

"What do you think? Should we say Mrs. Horvath's opinion is another neutral one?"

"Sure," Jared replied. "So one more."

"Finally, for another not-very-Orthodox perspective, I called Rabbi Meyer at Beth Shalom. Remember, he married your Uncle Gary and Aunt Gracie. He's the Reform rabbi."

"He's at the temple with all the prayers in English, right?"

"Well, they do repeat a lot of the prayers in English, right. Nice man. To his way of thinking, you should go. He said, If it truly means that much to your son—and I told him it certainly does—then why not? We all need all the blessings we can get, he says. It wouldn't hurt to let him go, while maybe keeping your son from going would hurt."

"Why don't we go to *his* shul? Sounds nicer."

"And leave your great-grandparents, who only helped to start our shul? And drive forty-five minutes each way to Hebrew school? Or—"

"I was just joking, sort of. So he'd be in favor of my going."

"Yes, and, I have to admit, there's something I also like about the all-the-blessings-you-can-get philosophy."

Jared and his mother jogged down the shoreline to catch up with Shayna, who had finally found her duck. Every time they visited the lake, Shayna and one water bird or another performed this same routine: The dog seemed determined to swim to the horizon and beyond if necessary to chase the duck, and the duck, for its part, would let Shayna follow until the dog came within a few yards, and then, in a splash, the bird would dive and disappear. Next, Shayna would swim

in spirals, whether baffled or just guessing where the duck might reappear, until, a few moments and several yards later, the duck would resurface somewhere and the chase would begin again. Unless the duck decided to call it quits and fly away, or Jared managed to grab the dog's attention again, Shayna looked as though she'd swim all night and day.

Watching this game, seeing how the duck obviously accepted its role in the chase, and how the dog probably knew there was no possibility of catching the bird, Jared thought of Rabbi Silver's words. These two animals, at least, clearly lived within some predictable plan: God's.

"And now your turn," his mother prompted. "What did you find out? I heard you talked to your father— good, good—and he said he saw you and Rabbi Silver sprinting past the parking-lot windows and talking."

Jared alternated shouts to Shayna with bits of his report: one, his father's yes, if only to be fair; two, Pappap's sort of no, be proud instead; three, Mr. Goldfarb's sort of no, bad question; and four, Rabbi

Silver's . . . well, Rabbi Silver's complicated answer. Though Shayna did listen to Jared and turned toward shore each time he called, whenever the duck honked or flapped, Shayna took that as the next command and paddled back toward the duck.

By the time Jared and his mother had circled that section of the lake, Shayna joined them at the car; her duck was nowhere to be seen. Jared grabbed the towel his mother had remembered and set to drying the dog's coat. Shayna stared up at him, her grinning gums brilliant red from all the exertion, her tongue lolling from the side of her mouth as she panted. "*What* a good girl, *what* a duck chaser, *what* a beautiful Shaynalayna!" Jared rubbed the towel along her long, dripping coat, praising and praising the Lab for—well, not for doing anything, really, but just for *being* something. Being a dog. *His* dog.

"Well, you've got a lot to consider," Jared's mother said as the car doors shut and Jared buckled in. "Not exactly eight answers, but plenty of interesting ideas, don't you think? I promised: I'm not going to tell you what to do. *I'm* not going, of course—even though you said parents *were* invited."

Jared just stared at his mother, realizing the discussion was finally over and that now, in the next few days, he'd have to make up his mind. He did know that he wanted to tell his mother "thank you," but he wasn't sure for what. Just for letting him argue with her all week? For making him get all those opinions? But then the car turned into the Dairy Freeze drive-thru at the entrance to the lake, and instead, he leaned across his mother to order. "One chocolate cone," he called to the voice behind the menu speaker. "And one vanilla cone—"

"Put that vanilla in a cup. And one root-beer float," his mother added, winking at Jared. "Why not? If you two are having a treat, the driver surely deserves one today, too."

# BLESSINGS AT LAST

True to her word, for the rest of the school week, Jared's mother said nothing further about the St. Francis Festival. Even Jared had ceased worrying about it. He had made his decision, so until Saturday morning, it was business as usual: breakfast, packing lunch, school, homework (including more stupid geometry), Hebrew tutor (Tuesday and Thursday), Shayna's obedience class (Wednesday), suppers with his mother, walks with Ian and Bellow, riding his bike to the library to borrow some movies, school reading, free-time reading, bed, dreams.

.      .      .

The Blessing of the Animals was scheduled for three o'clock: first Father Tim's blessing, then outside for the parade around St. Catherine's block, and then, after the animals had been taken home, back inside for the potluck.

From his third-floor window, which peered over the yard's tall magnolia, Jared and Shayna could see the entire front lawn of St. Catherine's. People had already begun to decorate the grounds before he had awakened. A dozen teenagers—some youth group, Jared figured, with matching T-shirts—were assembling cardboard litter boxes (not for cats, for trash) and depositing them around the property. And one person was placing a box of sandwich bags beside each one.

Then the littlest kids and a few taller parents trooped out, twirling and waving construction-paper chains and twisted crêpe-paper garlands to festoon the trees. Others stationed stainless-steel dog bowls (mixing bowls, really) all over the just-mowed lawn; from

Jared's vantage, they appeared like a new constellation, sparkling from sunlight and from the water sloshed up to their rims.

Two long horse trailers had parked on the street, but no horses had yet appeared. And there was a pickup truck parallel-parked, with a pig in it that filled its entire flatbed. Jared recognized Lindsey Cooper in the cab and guessed that the pig might be her 4-H project. But horses and pigs weren't going into the church—even the social hall part. That Jared knew for sure. Maybe just being near the church was close enough to receive the blessing, or maybe Father Tim made a quick round of outside blessings before the parade. Then Jared saw a man setting up a speaker, so he figured that's how the priest's message would reach the outdoors.

Later, another group of children hung suet-and-seed bells and paper-carton bird feeders on low branches, as though migrating birds might have scheduled a layover for the blessing and planned to stay and eat, too.

A few other horse trailers—not all filled with horses, as it turned out—wedged into the church lot, and by two o'clock the church's blacktop was crammed full. Cars began to circle the block for parking slots—in most, a dog's head was framed in one window, panting.

Some people had brought bowls of tropical fish. Jared could pick them out easily: they were the ones crossing *very* slowly toward the low, wide steps where the crowd was entering. Jared had counted at least twenty-six different breeds of dogs, and plenty of mixed breeds. As for the cats, most hid inside carriers, although, occasionally, he spotted a brave cat in its owner's arms; Jared could almost hear the hissing as one of the less trained canines tugged too close.

And then bird cages, rabbit cages, those terrariums with plastic trails for gerbils and hamsters, and shoe boxes and cardboard boxes with who-knows-what inside—insects? hermit crabs? tarantulas? Some boy stood outside hugging an inflatable *Tyrannosaurus rex* that was twice his size. Jared asked Shayna, "I don't think St. Francis was around in the dinosaurs' days, do you?"

Teddie Lavelle had even brought his nine-foot boa constrictor, which Jared remembered from Teddie's science-fair display at school. Although the area in front of St. Catherine's steps was now packed with people waiting to be let inside, Teddie and Stretcher had their own wide circle of grass.

After an exceptionally long walk and a good brushing, Shayna had spent most of the afternoon in the apartment. But now the barking of all the visiting dogs had her whimpering and whining. Jared brought her downstairs and out onto the steps at the end of the path that trailed through Mrs. Lewison's flower borders.

"Hi, Linda. Hi, Mrs. Cameron. You guys don't have any pets, do you?" Jared said to a late-coming family who lived two houses away.

Linda wore pigtails and a flouncy yellow dress that

even Jared recognized as a little girl's Easter outfit. She dropped her mother's hand to hold a poster board up over her head so Jared could see her drawing of a camel. No matter what she said, her voice rose in a question. "In our kindergarten at St. Catherine's? our class colored the animal we wanted most of all? so Father Tim could give a blessing to those?"

"Oh. I see," Jared said, and indeed, now that he knew what he was looking at, a number of poster boards popped out of the crowd at St. Catherine's. He had already noticed dozens of stuffed animals, too: giraffes, panda bears, lions, flamingos, hippos, porpoises. "I guess you don't really need a real animal for the blessing."

"Of course not," Mrs. Cameron replied. "Look around. Some people bring photos of pets that have passed away. See over there? Kind of sad and sweet at the same time." Jared's eyes followed to where her finger pointed. Around the base of the largest oak, people had leaned framed photographs of their pets, some of them almost life-size. Photos of Jared's family's own deceased cats and dogs hung in the hallway outside their kitchen.

"Cassandra? this friend I know?" Linda reported. "She's bringing all the wood animals? in her Christmas nativity scene? also for the blessing?"

"Well, thanks for explaining," Jared said as Linda and her mother headed across the street. "But—oh yeah. Linda? You'd really want a *camel* most of all? They're mean and they spit."

"Nuh-uh. Not mine. Mine wouldn't," she said, quite sure of herself.

Jared and Shayna remained on the steps, the dog wedged between his knees—her favorite place—watching the stragglers file into the church. As long as she could oversee it all, Shayna didn't seem to mind these once-a-year-visitor dogs sniffing *her* privet hedge, *her* lamppost, *her* lawn at St. Catherine's—*hers*, at least until her family moved back to the country.

"What do you think, Shayna?" Jared said to himself, although the good thing about having Shayna was that Jared could say that out loud, directly to Shayna,

knowing full well that she wouldn't give him an answer (as his mother or father would) that he'd have to obey—or argue with, anyway. That wasn't the best part about having a dog, but it was one of the good parts. "You didn't really want to just stand around, all crowded in, with a bunch of stuffed animals and posters and weirdo snakes and strange dogs, did you? No, we don't, do we?"

"Hey, Jared!" Ian yelled from across the street. "Father Tim's going to start real soon. What are you waiting for?" Ian and Bellow dashed across the street and up the lawn. Shayna sniffed her friend a few times, then sat back down. But Ian's retriever barked nonstop, one *awruff* after another, as if now he were counting down the seconds until the ceremony began. "Come on, you guys can stand with us—we're with Randy and Joaquim and their families, too. Right near the water fountain."

"You go on. We're going to stay at home. It's fun just watching from here. Plus I can hear Father Tim's voice on the loudspeakers—except for when Bellow's barking."

Ian yanked his dog's leash, which interrupted the noise for about a second. "How come? You should be in the parade, at least. Won't your mom let you?"

"Yeah, she'd let me."

"I thought you were all psyched to come. I thought you said— Bellow! *Shut! Up!*"

"I was psyched. I am. I mean, being Jewish doesn't mean I can't come. I'll explain it all later; you'll understand."

"Okay, come on, then. You're already missing part of the fun. Shayna will be left out."

"No, it's fine," Jared said, and realized that he honestly didn't want to get Shayna blessed, and what's more, he didn't feel the slightest bit bad about that. "Shayna had a lot of blessings today—every day. See, Jewish people believe . . ."

Ian held his hands loosely around Bellow's muzzle to stop the barking. "What'd you say? I missed what you were saying."

"I said, Shayna—and Bellow, and all dogs—they *come* blessed, see—"

"*Shut! Up! Bellow!* Look, whatever. I don't want to miss the start," Ian concluded, since Bellow had pulled his head free and resumed the barking countdown as they maneuvered toward the street. "Just join in for the parade—or I'll come over afterward," Ian shouted. "Come on, *quit!* Stupid dog! *Quiet!*"

"Ian, how come you just don't come to obedience class with us? Golden retrievers are really fast learners," Jared replied and then, in a louder voice, added, "So come over afterward."

Jared turned and walked into the house, leaping two steps at a time up to the third-floor window overlooking Ian and Bellow and a few other late arrivals rushing toward the church entrance. Jared's own lucky dog bounded into the room ahead of him, where Jared's mother had been watching, too, or maybe waiting for her son.

"I just want you to know, young man, I'm *not* proud of you for *not* going," she said, reaching her open arms toward Jared.

"You're not?"

"No, I'm just plain proud of you." Jared let his mother hug him an extra-long time. "I was worried about you. Just a little. I know this was hard."

"No, I'm fine. Shayna's disappointed, even though she says she isn't. So I promised her we'd take her duck-chasing every day next week. Okay?"

"Good!" his mother replied. "I'll quit my job so I can devote the rest of my days just for her pleasure!"

The loudspeakers at St. Catherine's crackled to life, and Father Tim's voice boomed out the church windows and doors, across the lawn, across the animals waiting in the trailers and the flatbed trucks, across the streets, and into the neighboring homes' open windows. *"Testing, testing, testing."* All three of them—Jared, his mother, and Shayna—scrunched down, huddling together at the high window, where, even if they couldn't see the blessing, they would feel it in the air, as though Father Tim's words were part of the cool breeze, just another piece of the Almighty's natural plan that Rabbi Silver had described.

"Oh, speaking of testing," Jared's mother added, "I'm trying out a new recipe for apple crisp with those apples you brought home. It's got pecans *and* oatmeal in the topping. I thought, just in case you did decide to go to the Festival, that maybe you should have something for the potluck."

"Really? You did? Well, maybe . . ." Jared was so surprised he wasn't sure what to reply. "I guess we could just eat it ourselves, or what about if Ian's family came over afterward to have some?" He leaned over to plant a kiss on his mother's cheek, and Shayna, not to be left out, added her own lick.

"Well, they'll probably be full from the potluck and won't want yet another dessert. How about this? How about if we watch the parade from here," his mother continued, "which has to be the best seat in the neighborhood, and then when folks return later for the potluck, you and I just go on over and join in the eating part."

"You mean it, Mom? You'd come, too? I mean,

you're right, it wouldn't be religious or anything, just eating with our friends and all, like at a wedding reception or something, right? And we could—"

"Sure, we could! I bet you that Pappap and both rabbis and the cantor and Mr. Goldfarb—I bet you everyone we talked to would give their blessing to sharing food with friends."

"Mom, that's the best! It's perfect. It's getting to be Jewish but also knowing about Shayna being blessed without Father Tim, but I get to go to the Festival just like another neighborhood family—"

"Slow down, slow down. Next thing, you'll want me to call Dad and see if he'll drive to town and join in, too."

"That would be great, but he's not— You wouldn't just call him now. He's probably busy."

"No, actually, he'll be here by five, he said. He's got to stop and pick up Pappap and Grams first."

"No! Now I know you're kidding."

Up until then, the window had brought them phrases of Father Tim's speech: ". . . brother to all creatures . . ." and ". . . creation is the language of God's thoughts . . ." and ". . . gentle spirits that share our world . . ." But suddenly a song—hundreds of voices and at least one howling dog—lifted up from the social hall at St. Catherine's. While the words were jumbled in the distance, the tune was almost recognizable.

"You know that song, don't you?" his mother asked. "That's 'Bless the Beasts and the Children.' You used to sing it at camp."

"When I was little, I guess. But, Mom, are Dad and everyone really coming?"

"Yep. We've been meaning to have a get-together here, anyway, and— No, the truth is, they all wanted to be a part of your day today. Family's a blessing, too, Jared, even if your dad and I haven't figured out exactly how we refit ourselves into God's plan."

"But you could figure it out. You could try harder. You like Dad. It's not as though you guys don't even speak, like Aunt Cynthy and Uncle Jason."

"Wait, wait. Too many things. One thing at a time.

Your father and I are trying. We are, but I'm not going to just hug you and tell you it's all fixed. It might never be fixed. Want a hug, anyway?"

"No. No more hugging until we move back to the orchard with Dad."

"You are impossible," his mother announced, and grabbed Jared in a bear hug. "So let's do today. Your father's bringing cider, and Grams is bringing noodle kugel—Pappap thought it was sort of funny to sneak a Jewish dish into the potluck."

"Pappap said that?"

"You know, one taste of her fabulous kugel could make some people convert . . ."

The church microphone fell silent, and almost immediately the people closest to the door stepped outside, squinting in the brilliant sunshine. Dogs resumed barking. The kindergartners marched out of the hall with their animal posters raised high over their heads like some prehistoric caterpillar. The patient horses were led from the trailers onto the sidewalk, where the parade line was to form. There stood Father Tim at the head, with his white robe, speaking to four policemen who had arrived to redirect the traffic. And then Shayna's ears pricked up at the sound of Bellow's voice. There was Ian waving up at them from the crowd. Or maybe waving them to come down.

Just then, inside Jared's apartment, from the downstairs kitchen, the timer on the stove began to buzz. "The apple crisp's ready," his mother announced, and headed for the stairs.

Outside, the parade continued to assemble. To Jared, peering over the jumble of people and animals, it looked like a scene at Noah's ark when the animals finally get to leave the ship, kind of cranky and stiff and a little lost, but really happy to be back on land. The crowd at St. Catherine's certainly wasn't walking two by two, the way all those pictures and songs describe the flood. Two by two? No, in real life, Jared thought as he knelt to watch the parade, things like animals—and parents, and even decisions—don't always come in simple pairs.